The BLUE FAIENCE HIPPOPOTAMUS

By Joan Grant ~ Illustrated by Alexandra Day

A STAR & ELEPHANT BOOK
The Green Tiger Press

Illustrations copyright ©1984 by Alexandra Day.
Text copyright ©1942 by Methuen & Co. Ltd.;
copyright ©1984 by Joan Grant.
Story originally published in *The Scarlet Fish and Other Stories*
by Joan Grant. London: Methuen & Co. Ltd., 1942.
First Edition ◆ First Printing
ISBN 0-88138-020-2
THE GREEN TIGER PRESS
La Jolla ◆ London

On an island of the Nile, just before you come to the First Cataract, there once lived a princess, the youngest daughter of Pharaoh. She had caused a house to be built there because she was not happy in her father's palace: he was an old and stupid man, unworthy to wear the Double Crown, and his two elder daughters and his three sons were nearly as unpleasant as their father. But the youngest princess was kind, and very beautiful, and the friend of laughter.

When she was fifteen she left the Royal City and journeyed upriver in search of a place where she could live undisturbed by her difficult relations. With her came her old nurse, two female servants, a gardener, a stonecutter, and five rowers. The gardener could row as well as garden, and the stonecutter had learned how to steer, from his father who was a fisherman, so they made quite good progress, and on the twenty-third day of their journey they reached the island.

Two of the rowers were married to the female servants, the third was apprenticed to the stonecutter, and the fourth and fifth soon became so interested in laying out a garden, under the direction of the gardener, that they had little time for anything else. The nurse was old, and still apt to treat the Princess as though she were a small child. So the Princess, having no one to play with, was often very lonely.

On three sides the island had steep banks, but on the fourth it shelved gently down to the water, and it was here the Princess used to bathe every morning. Now the pool in which she bathed was the favorite haunt of a certain Hippopotamus; and the Princess looked so beautiful swimming about in the water, or lying on the warm rocks to get dry again, that the Hippopotamus fell in love with her.

This made him very unhappy, for he knew there was no hope of a princess falling in love with a Hippopotamus. Every day she seemed more and more beautiful, and every day the Hippopotamus became more and more unhappy because he wasn't a suitable shape for a princess to fall in love with. He was getting so thin with unhappiness that his skin was several sizes too large for him. Then, one day, he heard two herons talking to each other while they were waiting for fish to mistake their legs for reeds. (Whether fish do mistake heron's legs for reeds I don't know, but herons think they do.)

One of the herons was talking with his beak full, so he sounded rather mumbly, but the Hippopotamus heard him say something about, "Magician who lives in...cave...beyond Third Cataract."

Then the heron swallowed, and said more intelligibly, "I've never seen him myself, but he is said to be able to turn a giraffe into a butterfly, or a frog into a gazelle, so great is his magic."

"I don't think that's so very clever," said the other heron. "I can change an egg into a heron just by sitting on it, and a chrysalis can change itself into a butterfly without anyone helping at all!"

The Hippopotamus rose up out of the water, for he wanted to ask the herons a lot of important questions about where the Magician lived. But the herons were annoyed at having their fishing disturbed, so they flew away without answering.

"Beyond the Third Cataract," said the Hippopotamus to himself. "I've never been farther than the Second Cataract, and that was in my grandfather's time. But if I stay in the river and walk against the current I shall find the Third Cataract. 'In a cave,' they said. I shall easily know *which* cave if I watch carefully. For if I see butterflies going in and giraffes coming out (or the other way round), I shall know that is the doorway to the Magician's house."

So the Hippopotamus set off upriver, and by the beginning of the next season he came to the Third Cataract; and beyond the Third Cataract he came to a cave. He looked carefully to see if there were any giraffes about, but all he could see was a butterfly, which had a surprised look on its face as though it might quite easily have been a much

larger animal only a few moments before.

The Magician was stringing crocodiles' teeth together to make a fur-lined cloak—which isn't so very improbable if you're a magician; they often find it easier to do things in apparently difficult ways.

The Magician seemed not to notice the Hippopotamus, who coughed, rather shyly, to draw his attention.

"Needn't cough. Knew you were there," said the Magician crossly. "What do you want? Make up your mind. If you don't want anything, don't interrupt."

"Oh, but I *do* want something!" said the Hippopotamus. "Most certainly I do. And I've come a long way."

"Everything has come a long way," said the Magician. "It is only a question whether it goes backwards or forwards. With the current or against it."

"Oh, I went against the current all the way; otherwise I shouldn't have found you."

"Silly. Makes it more difficult. Still, now you're here you may as well tell me why you came."

"It's rather difficult to explain," said the Hippopotamus, rubbing his knees together nervously, which was a habit he had when he was feeling shy.

"Go on. Hurry up. Can't you see I'm busy?" snapped the Magician.

The Hippopotamus gulped, and said all in a rush, "Please change me into something that a princess can fall in love with."

For the first time the Magician seemed really interested. He put down the necklace of crocodiles' teeth, which immediately changed into a cloak of water rat skins neatly stitched together....Part of the hem of the cloak wasn't there because two crocodile teeth were still unthreaded.

"Something that a princess could fall in love with? That's interesting. Very interesting indeed."

"Do you think you could manage it?" asked the Hippopotamus.

"Of course. Don't ask silly questions. If you don't believe in me, go to another magician."

"But I *do* believe in you," said the Hippopotamus fervently. "Even if I had any doubts in the first place—which I hadn't—I should have had complete faith in your powers when I saw that surprised butterfly outside your door. Was it a giraffe that you had turned it out of?"

"Observant of you. Very," said the Magician in a much more genial voice. Then he added modestly, "Not a giraffe, though. Frog. Easy magic. Usually leave things like that to the apprentices. They've both got stomach ache from eating too much. Taught them how to turn rocks into cake. They ate two boulders before I remembered to stop them. Never mind. Teach them a lesson. Good thing."

"Then," said the Hippopotamus diffidently, "you wouldn't mind changing me into a prince?"

"Prince? No. Can't do that. Sorry. Gave up mixing humans and animals two years ago. Complications. Caused trouble."

A large tear ran out of the Hippopotamus's right eye and splashed on the floor.

"Stop snivelling," said the Magician sharply. "Lots of things beside princes that princesses can love."

The Hippopotamus scuffled a little sand over the wet patch his tear had made, and said cautiously, "What *kind* of things?"

"That depends on what kind of princess. Is she greedy? If so, could turn you into a cake."

"Oh no," said the Hippopotamus hastily, "not at all greedy."

"Pity. Can't be helped. Does she covet gold?"

"I don't think so, otherwise she would have stayed in her father's palace."

"Probably. What about face paint?"

"I'm afraid I don't quite understand." By now the Hippopotamus was beginning to feel rather bewildered.

"Stupid. Is she afraid of losing her beauty? Most women are. Could turn you into face paint. Easy job. Malachite if you prefer it, though the grinding might be uncomfortable."

"*Not* malachite," said the Hippopotamus firmly.

"I've had three ideas. Now you have one."

"I think she needs something to *play* with. I'm so big that I might frighten her, and anyway her nurse is a stupid person who thinks Hippos are dangerous animals. I heard her say so."

"A toy. That's what you'd better be. Small enough to carry about and not so small that you'd get lost. What shape do you prefer?"

"I don't want to sound conceited," said the Hippopotamus bashfully, "but I always think that Hippos are really the very nicest shape. Too large, and perhaps not a very interesting color, but a very nice shape."

"Gold? Silver? Ivory? What do you want to be made of?"

"I think blue is her favorite color. Could you manage a nice blue?"

"Faience. That's what you'd better be. It's a better color than turquoise, or lapis, in my opinion. Much more uncommon, too."

Suddenly the Magician seemed to grow twenty times as tall as he had been a moment before, and the cave, which until then had seemed rather small and stuffy, now looked so large that the Hippopotamus could only just see to the sides of it. And the Magician's voice sounded as loud as a cataract, though not nearly so deafening, when he said, "Nice job. Very nice job indeed. Fine glaze. Not a flaw in it anywhere."

Then the Magician carried the blue faience Hippopotamus out of the cave so that it could look at itself in a pool of water.

"Is that really me?" asked the Hippopotamus in a very small voice.

"Course it is. Doesn't it feel like you?"

"I'm not sure what me feels like when it's so small. Are you *sure* the Princess will love me like this?"

"Certain of it. There's not another one like you in all Egypt."

"How shall I get back to the Princess?"

"Easy. Trader comes downriver from the Land of Gold every season. Often buys things from me. Shall tell him to sell you to the Princess."

Suddenly the Hippopotamus had a frightening thought.

"Suppose she *doesn't* buy me!"

"She will. Bound to."

"But if she doesn't?"

"You can use your wish.'

"What wish?"

"The wish I give away with every magic. You can use it whenever you like. If she doesn't buy you, say, 'I wish to be back in my ordinary pool in my ordinary

size'...better add 'ordinary color' too, just to be on the safe side. Can't be too careful with magic. Then you'll be no worse off than you were before, and a lot wiser."

The sound of a hail came from somewhere upriver, and the Magician said, "That's the trader. Nice timing. You'd better stop talking...not that he'd understand you of course. Nothing except magicians will understand you as long as you're in that shape. Except the same kind of things as you are."

Then the Magician wrapped the blue faience Hippopotamus in a piece of fine linen, and before putting him into the trader's boat he whispered, "Don't forget to say, 'In my usual pool' before you say 'In my usual size,' when you use your wish. Otherwise it would work at once, wherever you happened to be. You'd sink the boat. Bad for the trader. Can't have that. Friend of mine."

The Magician went back into his cave, and the trader set course downriver: and the little blue faience Hippopotamus cowered inside his wrappings of fine linen and tried not to feel frightened.

He soon began to feel more cheerful, and he found that one of the advantages of being made of faience instead of ordinary hippopotamus is that you never feel hungry. Then he began to wonder whom he would find to talk to, for the Magician had said, "Only those of your own kind will understand you." But he had also said,

"You are the only one of your kind in all Egypt."

The Hippopotamus knew when he came to a cataract, for everything was taken out of the boat and carried down the path to below the angry water; and the third time this happened he knew he was approaching the island. Then he felt the boat jar against the landing place, and he was lifted out and carried up some steps and into the dayroom of the Princess.

The sound of voices, muffled by the linen in which he was still wrapped, came to his small, round ears. And he was surprised and delighted to find that, although he couldn't talk, he could

understand even better than when he had been an ordinary hippopotamus. Then he felt the wrappings being taken off, and he was put on a cedarwood chest beside the chair on which the Princess was sitting.

When she saw him she cried out excitedly, "Of course I must have him. I've never seen anything I liked half so much!"

She picked him up, and stroked him, and held him against her cheek. He felt light as a bubble of joy; and if he had had a heart it would have beaten so fast that it would probably have cracked his glaze.

For the next few days she took him everywhere with her, even down to the river when she went to bathe, and when she was eating he sat on a stool beside her. Yet after a while, though she quite often remembered to pat him, she left him on the toilet table in her bedroom. And for most of the day he was lonely, listening for her footsteps.

It was one of these lonely times when he heard a voice say, "Are you still too proud to speak to us?"

And to his surprise he realized that the voice was coming from an ivory palette, on which the Princess mixed oil and malachite to make her eye paint.

"Surprised, aren't you?" said the voice again. "I suppose you thought you have to look like an animal before you can speak like an animal. Well, I was an animal once: an elephant with tusks four cubits long. Hunters killed me. I was thinking about my wife and never noticed the trap they had made until I had fallen into it. They thought I was dead; they didn't know I was still living in one of my tusks. It must be a hundred years since that happened to me. I belonged to our Princess's grandmother...or perhaps it was her great-grandmother, I forget. They don't realize how much their beauty depends on my will. I decide how fine the malachite is to be ground: I can make their eyes mysterious as deep water, or dull and shallow as a puddle in a marketplace. I can soften the tears they weep, or make the eyes of an old woman reflect her youth...even if only for an hour. And I protect their sight, for without me the Veil of Dusk might afflict them, and grow thicker and thicker until it made them blind. She is a kind child, our present mistress, for I admit I am getting rather worn....Powdered malachite is hard stuff to stomach for more than a century. But she brought me with her when she came from her father's palace, and left behind her five other palettes, all of them new and in the latest fashion.''

The Hippopotamus sighed, a long and trembling sigh. ''You are very lucky to be able to do so much for her. I used to make her smile, but now she's almost forgotten me. You can look after her and protect her every day of her life.''

''Never mind!'' said another, deeper voice. It came from the casket of silver and cedarwood in which the Princess kept her necklaces. ''Never mind,'' it repeated. ''When you're as old as I am you won't expect a woman to smile at the same thing for more than a few days. The Palette thinks he's very old...he with only a century of years to count!''

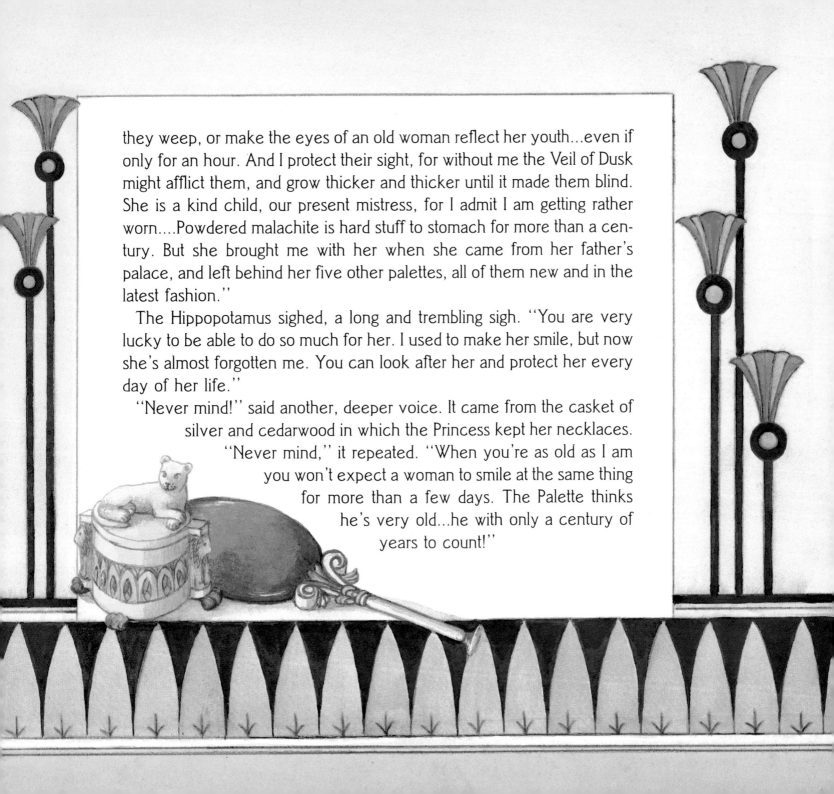

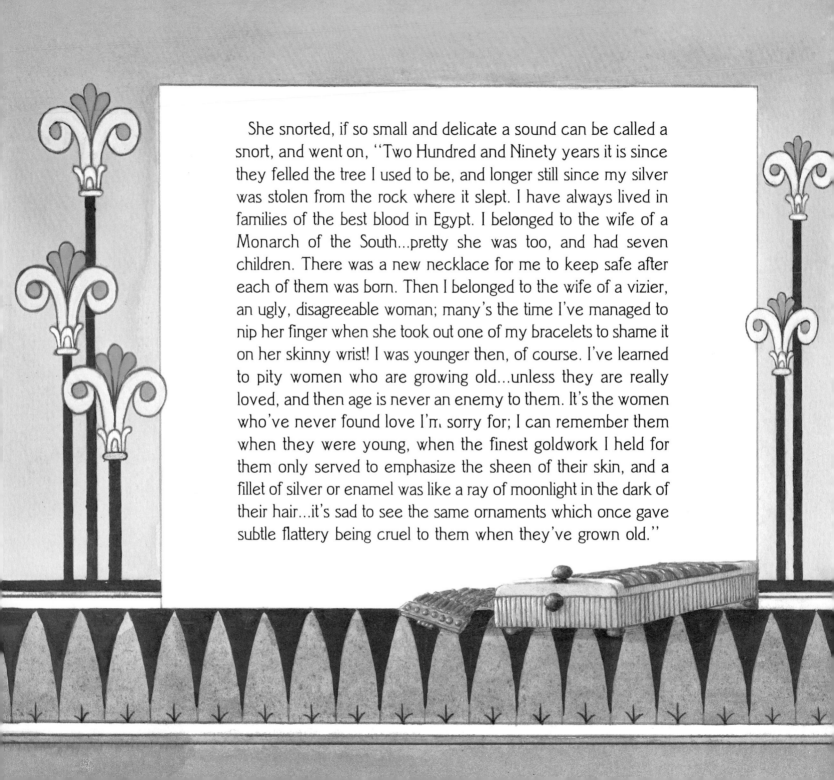

She snorted, if so small and delicate a sound can be called a snort, and went on, "Two Hundred and Ninety years it is since they felled the tree I used to be, and longer still since my silver was stolen from the rock where it slept. I have always lived in families of the best blood in Egypt. I belonged to the wife of a Monarch of the South...pretty she was too, and had seven children. There was a new necklace for me to keep safe after each of them was born. Then I belonged to the wife of a vizier, an ugly, disagreeable woman; many's the time I've managed to nip her finger when she took out one of my bracelets to shame it on her skinny wrist! I was younger then, of course. I've learned to pity women who are growing old...unless they are really loved, and then age is never an enemy to them. It's the women who've never found love I'm sorry for; I can remember them when they were young, when the finest goldwork I held for them only served to emphasize the sheen of their skin, and a fillet of silver or enamel was like a ray of moonlight in the dark of their hair...it's sad to see the same ornaments which once gave subtle flattery being cruel to them when they've grown old."

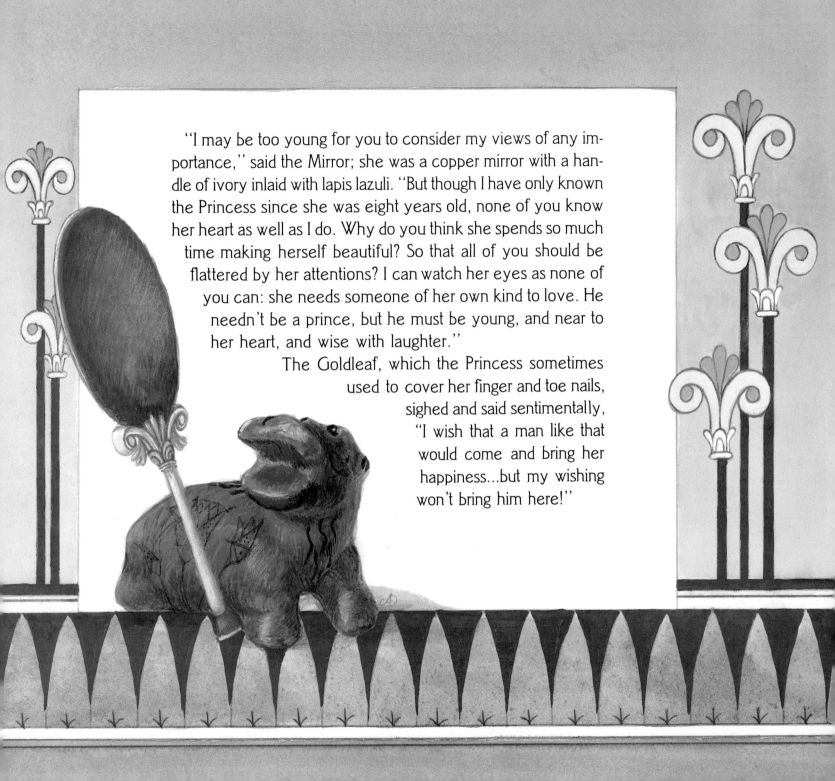

"I may be too young for you to consider my views of any importance," said the Mirror; she was a copper mirror with a handle of ivory inlaid with lapis lazuli. "But though I have only known the Princess since she was eight years old, none of you know her heart as well as I do. Why do you think she spends so much time making herself beautiful? So that all of you should be flattered by her attentions? I can watch her eyes as none of you can: she needs someone of her own kind to love. He needn't be a prince, but he must be young, and near to her heart, and wise with laughter."

The Goldleaf, which the Princess sometimes used to cover her finger and toe nails, sighed and said sentimentally, "I wish that a man like that would come and bring her happiness...but my wishing won't bring him here!"

The little Hippopotamus thought, "Her wishing won't. But mine...? The Magician said, 'The wish I give away with every magic.' The Magician thought I would use it to turn myself back into an ordinary hippopotamus....when I get too lonely without my family and tired of being made of blue faience.."

He decided it would need thinking about very carefully, for every day he was getting more lonely for the river. He wanted to know cool, deep water again; to feel the green squishy taste

of water plants under his tongue. Then there was that very beautiful female hippopotamus whom he had noticed several times. If he had never seen the Princess bathing he might have had a son to talk to by now, and perhaps a daughter as well. Yes, tomorrow he would use his wish on himself, not on anyone else. Tomorrow he would be basking in the sun, or feeling the water trickle past his ears as he lay half submerged in the middle of the river. Then there was the lovely, black, squelchy sound his feet made as he walked through the mud; he had almost forgotten that. Tomorrow he would know it all again.

It was long after sunset when the Princess came to bed, and she carried a lamp in her hand. She set it down on the toilet table between the Palette and the Hippopotamus. She stroked him gently with her forefinger and he felt a tear splash on his back.

"Dear little Hippopotamus," she said. "You are so lucky to be made of faience. You don't know what it feels like to be lonely; to be young where everyone else is old; to want to be gay where everyone else is serious! I thought that when I ran away to this island a lover would come to find me. But I have watched the river for his boat through all the seasons of the year. There are very few boats, and they all go past the landing place. Yet I watch them until they are hidden by the bend of the river, in case one should turn back to find me.''

Then she put him down and blew out the lamp; and the little Hippopotamus heard her getting slowly and sadly into bed.

Soon everything in the room, including the Princess, was asleep; except the little Hippopotamus. He was wishing, and his wish was, ''May the man who belongs to the Princess's heart arrive here tomorrow morning, and may they be happy together for ever and ever.''

And because the Magician was the best kind of magician, the wish came true. The next morning a young noble came upriver in his pleasure barge of twenty oars. He saw the Princess bathing in the pool, even as the Hippopotamus had once seen her, and as soon as they saw each other they knew neither of them would ever be lonely any more.

And the only tears that the Princess ever shed after that day, were when a careless servant knocked the little blue faience Hippopotamus off the table...and he broke into twenty pieces.

When the Hippopotamus felt himself falling he knew he was going to be broken. But what he didn't know was that the very next moment he would find himself outside the cave of the Magician.

The Magician said, "I made the servant drop you. Had to. You are too old to be faience any more. You are the only one of my magics that didn't use its wish for itself. Worth ten thousand years is a wish like that. Saved yourself a lot of trouble. Needn't be an animal any more. You are human. Needn't join one of the young tribes. You're ready to be born an Egyptian.

"You're the biggest magic I've ever done! Anyone can turn a butterfly into a giraffe, or an elephant into a water rat...But it takes a real magician to turn a hippopotamus into a..."

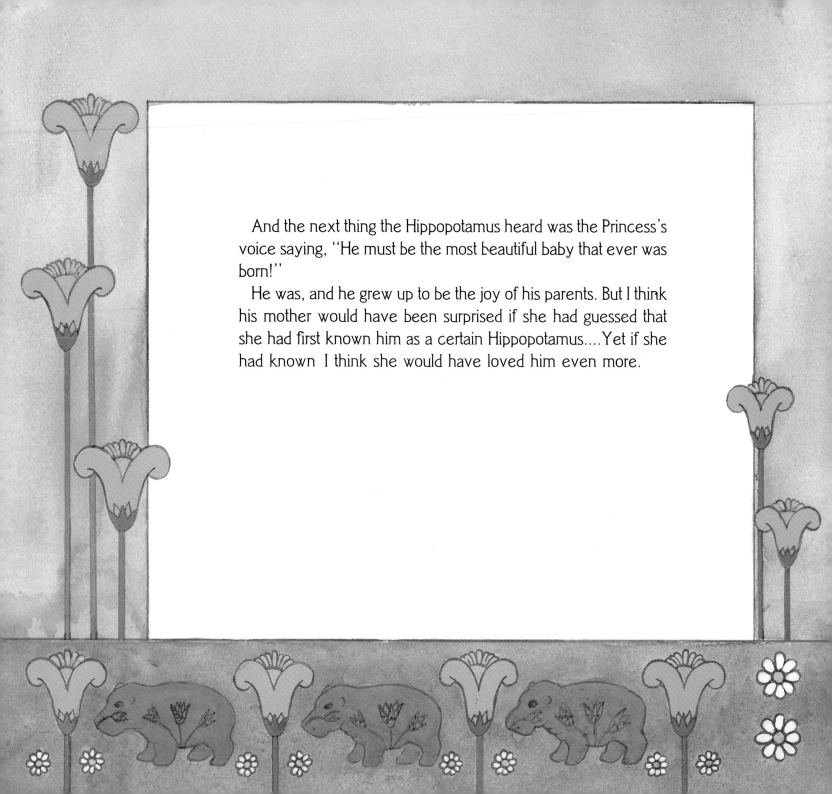

And the next thing the Hippopotamus heard was the Princess's voice saying, "He must be the most beautiful baby that ever was born!"

He was, and he grew up to be the joy of his parents. But I think his mother would have been surprised if she had guessed that she had first known him as a certain Hippopotamus....Yet if she had known I think she would have loved him even more.

THE ILLUSTRATIONS FOR THIS BOOK WERE PAINTED IN EGG TEMPERA.
COLOR SEPARATIONS ARE BY PHOTOLITHO AG, GOSSAU-ZURICH, SWITZERLAND.
TYPOGRAPHY, ENTITLED CAMELOT. IS BY TYPECAST OF SAN DIEGO, CALIFORNIA.
PRINTED AND BOUND BY WALTER-VERLAG AG, OLTEN, SWITZERLAND.